AUTHOR'S NOTE

In my day, toddler mealtime was supposed to be fun. According to my trusted authority, Dr. Spock, this would ward off eating problems later on. So I invented all sorts of little games to play before, during, and afterward. My son David especially loved the dump truck and choo-choo routine. But the runaway favorite with all three of my little ones was the "chin chopper" game. We did this endlessly—and not just at mealtime! I'd learned it from my grandmother—it was just one of many ancient folk rhymes she used to play with me. Here is how to do it:

"Eye winker"—Gently close left eye of child
"Tom tinker"—Gently close right eye of child
"Nose stopper"—Tug on the nose
"Mouth popper"—Poke food in child's mouth
"Chin chopper"—Tickle the chin

Another favorite feeding game of ours, not included in the book, goes like this:
"Knock on the door"—Tap on child's forehead
"Peek in"—Carefully open child's eyes wide
"Pull on the latch"—Tug on the nose
"Walk in"—Poke food in mouth
"Close the door behind you"—Hold on to chin and shut mouth

Have fun!   —N. V. L.

Atheneum Books for Young Readers
An imprint of Simon & Schuster
Children's Publishing Division
1230 Avenue of the Americas
New York, New York 10020

Text copyright © 2001 by Nancy Van Laan
Illustrations copyright © 2001 by Bernadette Pons
All rights reserved including the right of reproduction in
whole or in part in any form.

Book design by Lee Wade
The text of this book is set in Spectrum.
The illustrations are rendered in watercolor and soft pastels.
Printed in Hong Kong

2 3 4 5 6 7 8 9 10

Library of Congress Cataloging-in-Publication Data
Van Laan, Nancy.
Tickle tum! / by Nancy Van Laan ;
illustrated by Bernadette Pons. — 1st ed.
p.   cm.

"An Anne Schwartz book"
Summary: A mother and toddler have fun
at suppertime.

ISBN 0-689-83143-9

[1. Food habits—Fiction. 2. Mother and child—
Fiction. 3. Finger play.]
I. Pons, Bernadette, ill. II. Title.
PZ7.V3269 Ti 2001
[E]—dc21   99-047051

tickle tum!

by Nancy Van Laan
illustrations by Bernadette Pons

An Anne Schwartz Book
ATHENEUM BOOKS FOR YOUNG READERS
New York London Toronto Sydney Singapore

Uppa Uppa
time for suppa!

Up up high
touch the sky.

Way down there
munch-time chair.
Whirl aroundsy
sit sit downsy.

Tickle tickle tum tum
bidda bidda boo

lotsa super dooper stew
just for you.

Here comes
mama bird,
watch her glide.
Swoop down to
baby bird,
open wide!

Tickle tickle tum tum
giggle giggle goo
jolly jolly green bean
jumps to you.

Next comes a choo-choo

huff, puff, whoooooooo!

Chew, chew, chew it up

choo-choo stew.

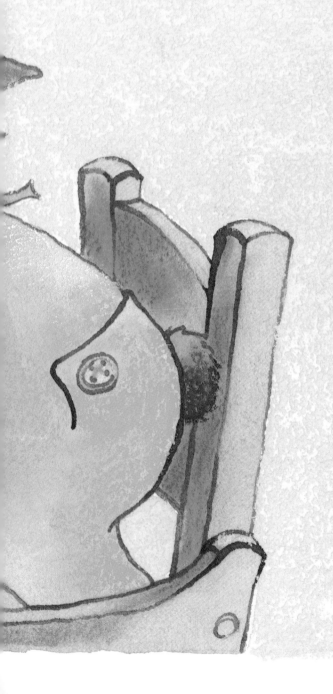

Eye winker
tom tinker
nose stopper
mouth popper.

Chin chopper
chin chopper
chin chopper.

Now comes a dump truck,
dumper full of peas.
Where shall it dump them?

In this mouth, please.

Tippa tip tat
slinga finga bat
peas roll across the
floor,

pounce goes the cat!

Squish squash squash squish

one bite

two bite

empty dish!

Fill up the tum, applesauce, yum!

Fulla fulla fum,

here I come.

Upsy upsy, done with suppsy.

Off you go, little bird,

up to your nest.

Time for
a nappy

so Mama
can rest.

Tickle tickle tum tum
bidda bidda boo

ticka ticka tumtee
I love you!